The THREE Little BUSH PIGS

For Aidan

Omnibus Books
335 Unley Road, Malvern SA 5061
an imprint of Scholastic Australia Pty Ltd (ABN 11 000 614 577)
PO Box 579, Gosford NSW 2250.
www.scholastic.com.au

Part of the Scholastic Group
Sydney • Auckland • New York • Toronto • London • Mexico City •
New Delhi • Hong Kong • Buenos Aires • Puerto Rico

First published in 2008.
Reprinted in 2008.
First published in this edition in 2010.
Reprinted in 2010, 2011.

National Library of Australia Cataloguing-in-Publication entry
Dallimore, Paul, 1971 – .
The three little bush pigs.
For pre-school age.
ISBN 978 1 86291 727 9.
I. Title.
A823.4

Typeset in GarthGraphic.
Scans by Graphic Print Group, Adelaide.
Printed in Singapore by Tien Wah Press (Pte) Ltd.

Scholastic Australia's policy, in association with Tien Wah Press, is to
use papers that are renewable and made efficiently from wood grown in
sustainable forests, so as to minimise its environmental footprint.

10 9 8 7 6 5 4 3   11 12 13 14 15 / 0

The THREE Little BUSH PIGS

Written and illustrated by Paul Dallimore

An Omnibus Book from Scholastic Australia

Deep in the Pilliga Scrub lived three little bush pigs who were as keen as mustard to leave home.

'Keep your eyes peeled for that dingrel,' said Dad.

'No worries,' said the three little bush pigs, and early the next morning they rode away.

The first little bush pig soon spotted a patch of prickly pear.

'Pull up here, fellas. I'm going to build my house out of prickly pear.'

'No way!' his brothers protested. 'You must be off yer rocker to build with that, you dag!'

'Whacko!' said the dingrel –
who had a head like a twisted
gumboot – when he spotted the
pigs. He was a bit of a slacker and
he liked an easy feed.

With an 'Ouch!' and an 'Oooh!' and an 'Aargh!' the first
little bush pig set to work to build his house out of
prickly pear.

Suddenly, out of the blue sprang the dingrel.

'I'll huff and I'll puff and blow your house away, maaaaaaaaaaaaaaaaaaaate!' he threatened.

But the first little bush pig wasn't afraid. 'I'm not going to be your dinny din-dins!' he squealed.

'You asked for it, you stinky hog!' And the dingrel sucked a huge gulp of air deep into his guts ...

and blew the prickly pear house halfway to Woop Woop, where the second little bush pig had just finished building a house out of Weet-a-Brix boxes.

'The dingrel is coming, the dingrel is coming!' cried the first little bush pig.

They both bolted inside just as the dingrel and his goanna mate Dazza rocked up in their ute.

'Oi! You stinky maggot bags!' growled the dingrel. 'Let me in, or I'll huff and I'll puff and blow your flippin' house away, maaaaaaaaaaaaaaaaaaaate!'

'No way, buster! We're not going to be your dinny din-dins!' sang the two little bush pigs.

So the dingrel huffed and he puffed ...

and blew the Weet-a-Brix house all the way to Woop Woop. The little bush pigs were sent flying to their sensible brother's place. He'd just finished building his mudbrick house, which had been approved in writing by the Pilliga Shire Council.

They all ran inside and locked the door.

The dingrel fanged it all the way to the third little bush pig's house.

The first two little bush pigs were scared spitless. 'Relax,' said the third little bush pig. 'He's full of it.'

The dingrel carried on like a real galah. He bragged and he boasted. He huffed and he puffed.

But in the end he was completely bushed!

That dimwit dingrel tried every single trick to get in the door.

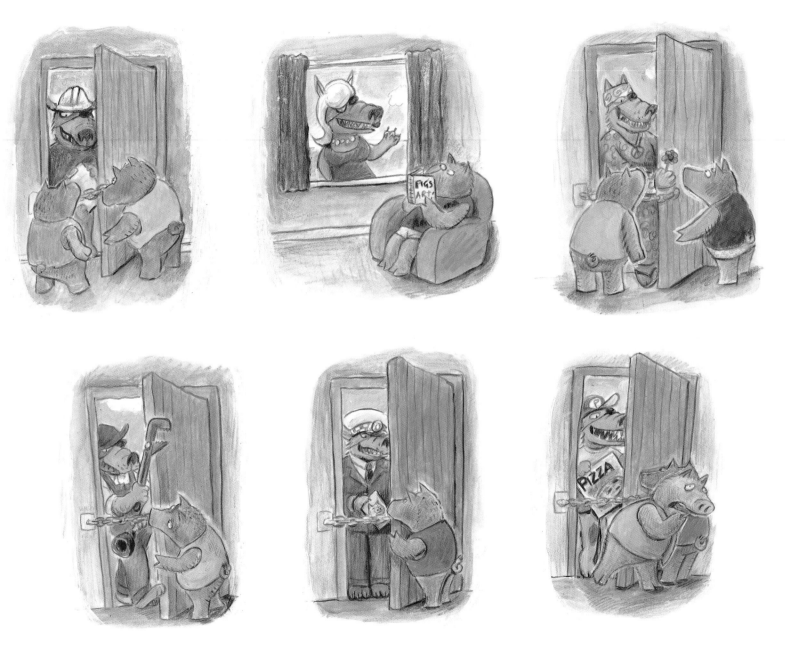

But the bush pigs weren't buying!

The dingrel needed a cunning plan. 'I know what I'll do,' he said. 'I'll hide in the wheelie bin. When the first little bush pig takes out the garbage, I'll jump out and grab him. And I'll get the second little bush pig and the third one the same way! One for soup, one for main course, and one for dessert. Yum!'

MENU

Ham and Pea soup
Pork and beans on toast
Pork scratchings
Pork surprise
Pork Pie
Pork strips in teriyaki marinade
Pigs in a blanket
Pork Pavlova
Pork with apple sauce and ice cream

The dingrel couldn't wait
for morning. But it was cosy
in the bin. It was so warm
that he fell asleep.

The bush pigs had been watching all the time. At the crack of dawn they sneakily and steadily wheeled out the wheelie bin.

When Roo's Rubbish removal truck arrived, the dingrel got quite a rude awakening ...

WOOOUUMPPP

AAAAAAAAAAAAH!

P.S.C.

'Hope you like your new home, stinky!'
giggled the bush pigs.

And most of the animals in this story
lived happily ever after.